PUFFIN BOOKS

A Bad Spell for the Worst Witch

Jill Murphy started putting books together (literally with
a stapler) when she was six. Her Worst Witch series, the
first book of which was published in 1974, is hugely
successful. She has also written and illustrated several
award-winning picture books for younger children.

A BAD SPELL FOR
THE WORST WITCH

JILL MURPHY

PUFFIN

PUFFIN BOOKS

Published by the Penguin Group
Penguin Books Ltd, 80 Strand, London WC2R ORL, England
Penguin Group (USA) Inc., 375 Hudson Street, New York, New York 10014, USA
Penguin Group (Canada), 90 Eglinton Avenue East, Suite 700, Toronto, Ontario, Canada M4P 2Y3
(a division of Pearson Penguin Canada Inc.)
Penguin Ireland, 25 St Stephen's Green, Dublin 2, Ireland (a division of Penguin Books Ltd)
Penguin Group (Australia), 707 Collins Street, Melbourne, Victoria 3008, Australia
(a division of Pearson Australia Group Pty Ltd)
Penguin Books India Pvt Ltd, 11 Community Centre, Panchsheel Park, New Delhi – 110 017, India
Penguin Group (NZ), 67 Apollo Drive, Rosedale, Auckland 0632, New Zealand
(a division of Pearson New Zealand Ltd)
Penguin Books (South Africa) (Pty) Ltd, Block D, Rosebank Office Park, 181 Jan Smuts Avenue,
Parktown North, Gauteng 2193, South Africa

Penguin Books Ltd, Registered Offices: 80 Strand, London WC2R ORL, England

puffinbooks.com

First published by Kestrel Books 1982
Published by Puffin Books 1988
This edition published 2014
001

Set in Baskerville
Printed in Great Britain by Clays Ltd, St Ives plc

British Library Cataloguing in Publication Data
A CIP catalogue record for this book is available from the British Library

ISBN: 978-0-141-35914-4

www.greenpenguin.co.uk

This book belongs
to

CHAPTER ONE

I t was the very first day of Mildred Hubble's second year at Miss Cackle's Academy for Witches.

The school year at the academy was divided into two long terms, the first of these commencing in September and stretching right to the end of January. This was known as the Winter Term and was followed by a month of welcome holiday. The second session began in

March and finished at the end of July, and this was called the Summer Term, though in fact it was still extremely cold and wintry when term began. Then there was another glorious month of holiday until the beginning of September, and the start of another year.

After her disastrous first year at the academy, it was something of a miracle that Mildred was returning there at all. She was one of those unfortunate people who seem to invite disaster wherever they go. Despite her efforts to be helpful and well-behaved, Mildred had an uncanny knack of appearing to be the cause of any trouble which was occurring, and it must be admitted that there *were* occasions (particularly when her rather wild imagination ran away with her) when she managed to turn some peaceful event into a scene of total chaos.

However, *this* year Mildred was older and hopefully wiser (at any rate she was

more full of good intentions than ever) and she was quite determined to lose her reputation as the worst witch in the school.

Arriving on her broomstick at the prison-like school gates, Mildred peered through the railings into the misty playground. For once she was early and there were only a handful of girls in the yard, all stamping their feet and huddling in their cloaks to keep out the bitter cold. It was always chilly at the school because the building was made of stone, rather like a castle, and was perched on the topmost peak of a mountain, surrounded by

pine trees which grew so close together that it was very damp and gloomy. In fact, the girls suffered permanently from colds and flu from all the time they were forced to spend in the freezing playground.

'Healthy fresh air!' Miss Drill, the gym mistress, would bark, herding the sneezing, coughing pupils outside. 'It'll do you all a power of good. Five hundred lines to anyone caught sneaking in before the bell!'

Mildred flew over the gates and landed expertly on the other side.

'Well, *that's* a good start!' she thought, looking around in the hope that someone had witnessed so successful a landing, but of course they hadn't. People were only ever watching when she did something dreadful, never at a moment of triumph.

Mildred took her suitcase from the back of the broomstick which was hovering politely, waiting for the next command. Then she turned her attention to the tabby cat still spreadeagled on the back of the broom with its eyes screwed tightly shut and its claws gripping on for dear life. The poor little cat had never got over its terror of flying, and Mildred always had to prise it from the broomstick whenever she arrived anywhere.

'Trust *me* to get a cat like you,' said Mildred fondly, stroking it with one hand and unclasping its claws with the other. 'Come on, silly, we're here. Look! It's all over, you can jump off now.'

The cat opened one eye cautiously, saw that it was true and sprang onto Mildred's shoulder where it rubbed its head gratefully against her hair. Mildred felt a wave of tenderness towards the scrawny creature.

'Mildred! Millie! It's *me*!' shrieked a familiar voice from above. Mildred looked up and saw Maud swooping over the gates, waving her hat in the air. This last action nearly caused her to fall off and she lurched to a rather drunken halt at Mildred's feet.

'Oh, Maud!' laughed Mildred, full of joy at the sight of her best friend after the long summer holiday. 'Gosh, you look a lot thinner, and your hair's got longer.'

'I know,' said Maud, stroking her hair

which was in two stubby plaits instead of her usual bunches. 'Mother put me on this *awful* diet. I wasn't allowed to eat *anything* except lettuce and celery and dreadful stuff like that. Still, I'm out of her clutches now, so it's back to good old school dinners. Three cheers for date-pudding and custard I say!' They both laughed.

'I don't know why they bother to *have* gates at this school,' remarked Mildred, as another three pupils soared over the wall on their brooms.

'Perhaps it's in case we have some ordinary visitors,' said Maud. 'You know, people who don't have brooms. Miss Cackle couldn't expect ordinary guests to bring ladders with them, could she? Who else has arrived, by the way? Anyone *we* know?'

'Only Ethel,' replied Mildred. 'She pretended not to see me though, not that I *care* of course.'

Ethel Hallow was the form sneak and goody-goody, and it was hardly surprising that Mildred felt unfriendly towards her after all the mean tricks Ethel had played during their first two terms, including almost getting Mildred expelled on two occasions.

'Oh look, Maud!' said Mildred, indicating two small girls in brand-new hats and huge cloaks which nearly touched their brand-new shining boots. 'They must be first-years, look at them. Don't they look *little*?'

'To think *we* were like that,' said Maud in a motherly way. 'It makes me feel quite old.'

The two first-years were standing close together, looking lost and shy. One of them was glancing nervously around, and the other was trying unsuccessfully to stop crying. They were a sorry-looking pair. Both were thin; the weeping one had a pinched, pale face and wispy mouse-coloured hair, and the other one had brilliant orange frizzy bunches. For some reason, the weeping one reminded Mildred very strongly of someone else, though she couldn't think who it was.

'Let's go and cheer them up, shall we?' suggested Mildred. 'They can't help being new, poor things. Remember how awful *we* felt?'

Feeling very grown-up and wise, Maud and Mildred sauntered casually over to the two pathetic little girls.

'Hello,' said Mildred, 'you must be new.'

'Yes,' chorused the girls.

Mildred patted the snivelling one awkwardly on the shoulder. 'Don't cry,' she said stiffly. 'It isn't *that* bad you know.' Unfortunately, Mildred's kindly gesture only served to make matters worse, instead of better, for the girl burst into deafening sobs and flung her arms round Mildred's waist.

Mildred was appalled. Everyone in the playground was staring at her, and any

minute now Miss Hardbroom (Mildred's terrifying form-mistress from the previous year) was bound to appear and accuse her of upsetting a poor new girl.

Maud detached the girl rather roughly and gave her a shake. 'Stop that silly noise at once!' she said crossly. 'You'll get Mildred into trouble before the first bell's even rung.'

Mildred smoothed her cloak. 'What's your name?' she asked.

'Sybil,' snuffled the girl.

'Mine's Clarice,' volunteered the other one.

'Are the teachers strict here?' asked Sybil, wiping her eyes with a corner of her voluminous cloak.

'Not really,' replied Maud.

'Well, Miss Hardbroom is,' said Mildred. 'In fact she's the worst of the lot, and she'll be *your* form-mistress. We're lucky this year because we'll get Miss Gimlett, and she's quite nice. But Miss

Hardbroom's horrendous. She just *appears* out of thin air –' At this point Mildred broke off and looked around in case she had done just that, but she hadn't.

'– *And* she says dreadful things to you in front of the whole class and makes you feel really stupid,' continued Maud.

'That's right,' said Mildred, 'and *I* heard tell that she changed *one* girl into a frog because she was two seconds late for a lesson. I don't know if it's true, but there *is* a frog sometimes seen near the pond in the backyard, and I've heard that it's *really* a poor first-year who –'

'I've never heard that before!' gasped Maud. '*Is* it true?'

'I *think* so,' answered Mildred, though in fact she had made up the tale on the spur of the moment and it had somehow got rather out of hand. To be honest, Mildred's stories often got rather out of hand, when she would find, to her dismay, that the whole class was listening and believing every word. She just *couldn't* say then that she'd made it all up.

Poor Sybil believed every word of Mildred's story about the frog and she burst into renewed and even noisier sobs, so deafening that Maud and Mildred thought it best to scurry away, leaving Clarice to offer comfort.

'Mildred! Maudie! Yoo hoo! It's *me*!'

Enid Nightshade, the new girl who arrived last term and was now their friend, came zooming over the treetops and screeched to a halt so forcefully that her cat and suitcase shot off the back, and

Maud and Mildred had to leap out of the way to avoid being run over.

At that moment the bell rang and the three witches picked up all their belongings and struggled inside with them.

'Thank goodness we haven't got H.B. any more,' whispered Enid. (H.B. was their nickname for Miss Hardbroom.)

'Yes,' agreed Mildred, 'this year should be as easy as pie without *her* breathing down our necks.'

CHAPTER TWO

The first announcement made by Miss Cackle at assembly was the ghastly news that Miss Hardbroom had changed places with Miss Gimlett, and would now be accompanying her old form into their second year. An audible groan rippled through the new Form Two, quelled at once by one of Miss Hardbroom's piercing glances which always made each pupil feel that they had been noticed personally.

With a sinking heart, Mildred moved miserably through all the chores of the first day, unpacking robes, arranging the new books in her desk, feeding the cat, and innumerable small tasks till at last it was bedtime.

The pupils were too depressed to bother sneaking into each other's rooms for a chat as they usually did on the first night back at school. Mildred lay in a glum heap under the blankets with the cat purring like a lawn-mower on her pillow, trying to think if there was any possible advantage in another year with Miss Hardbroom at the helm, but there wasn't.

Next morning, Mildred was jolted awake by the bell ringing in a much more frantic way than usual. It didn't take long for the cobwebs of sleep to clear and for her to realize that it was the fire-bell.

An untidily dressed Maud flung open Mildred's door as she rushed past. 'Quick,

Mil!' she shrieked. 'It's fire-drill, come on!'

'What a time to choose,' said Mildred, bundling on her tunic over her pyjamas. 'Perhaps it's a real fire?'

Maud went rushing off down the corridor, but Mildred stopped and looked out of the window to see if there was any evidence of fire. There, in the yard below, was Miss Hardbroom wreathed in thick purple smoke. She appeared to be standing in her customary arms-folded, upright posture, staring into the smoke as if she was in a trance, which seemed decidedly odd, given the circumstances.

'Crumbs!' thought Mildred. 'She's gone into a state of shock. I'll have to help!'

Mildred rushed to the washroom and seized the bucket which stood under the window there to catch drips from the leak in the ceiling. It was already half full with stagnant rain water, so Mildred filled it

to the brim, then carried it back to the yard window-sill, collecting her broomstick on the way.

She peered out of the window again, hoping that she might perhaps have imagined the scene below, but Miss Hardbroom had not moved and was now almost hidden from view by the smoke.

'Here goes!' said Mildred, her spirits rising as she thought how grateful her form-mistress would be. 'Perhaps I'll get a medal for bravery.'

It is difficult, at the best of times, to balance on a broomstick, but when you are trying to carry a heavy bucket of water at the same time, it is virtually impossible. Mildred did her best to arrange the bucket hanging from the back, but it was obviously going to spill the minute they took off, so she put the bucket back onto the window-sill, climbed onto the broom first, and then settled the bucket in her lap. This seemed

to be reasonably steady so, taking her courage in both hands, Mildred gave the word: 'Down, broom! Fast!'

Instantly they plunged into a vertical nose-dive so abrupt that the bucket flew from her grasp and dropped like a stone. Mildred swooped desperately after it but, alas, too late. A torrent of foul, icy water drenched Miss Hardbroom from head to toe, followed a second later by the bucket which crashed over her head with a doom-laden clang. To give the stern form-mistress some credit, it must be recorded that she did not flinch when the metal bucket struck, after falling from such a height.

Though her natural inclination was to turn round and zoom straight back again, Mildred could see that there was no escape. The smoke had cleared, revealing at least half the school lined up in rows and Miss Hardbroom still in the same position, with the bucket neatly over her head. For a mad moment, Mildred thought that perhaps, for some unknown reason, it was only a statue of Miss Hardbroom, but this illusion was shattered when the statue spoke.

'There is no need to ask *which* pupil is responsible for this,' came the familiar voice from inside the bucket. 'Mildred Hubble, perhaps you would be kind enough to assist me in my predicament?'

The sight of any other teacher dripping with water and with a bucket over her head would have been an occasion for great mirth among the pupils, but absolutely nothing could diminish Miss Hardbroom's power. Not a sound was heard,

not a smirk flickered on any face as Mildred stepped forward and stood on tiptoe to remove the bucket.

Miss Hardbroom's eyes bored into Mildred like a laser-beam the moment they came into view.

'Thank you, Mildred,' she said acidly.

'I – I'm s-sorry, M-M-Miss Hardb-b-broom,' gibbered Mildred, 'it was – I thought you were on fire – there was smoke so I, well I thought – it seemed . . .'

'Mildred,' said Miss Hardbroom heavily, 'does it seem likely to you that I would be standing here in the middle of a raging inferno, casually rounding up all you girls?'

'There was the smoke, Miss Hardbroom,' explained Mildred in a tiny voice, suddenly feeling aware of the striped pyjama legs under her tunic.

'*If* you remember your fire-drill, Mildred,' said Miss Hardbroom, 'pupils are expected in the yard through the main door, and *not*, as some girls seem to imagine, from the upstairs windows. On entering the yard through the *correct* entrance, they would have been met by me, who would then have informed them that the smoke was merely magic smoke to lend atmosphere to the proceedings and that there was no cause for total panic as some pupils would seem to be prone to.'

'Yes, Miss Hardbroom,' quavered Mildred, 'I'm sorry, Miss Hardbroom.'

'Get into line, Mildred,' ordered Miss Hardbroom. 'Let us just say that we expect this to be your only half-witted jape for the entire term. Ethel? Would you please fetch me a towel and my cloak before I turn into an iceberg?'

'Of course, Miss Hardbroom,' said Ethel, smiling demurely at her form-mistress, but pulling a horrid face at Mildred as she passed her by.

Mildred lined up next to her two friends, Maud and Enid.

'You are the limit, Mildred,' whispered Maud.

'I *know*,' said Mildred miserably. 'I must have been still asleep or something.'

'Actually,' said Enid, 'it was quite funny really.'

At this point all three friends felt an unruly wave of amusement sweeping over them, and the rest of the fire-drill was spent desperately avoiding each other's eyes in case a fit of the giggles should descend, and they were all agreed (especially Mildred) that this would definitely *not* be the thing to do.

CHAPTER THREE

Fire-drill was followed immediately by breakfast in the dining-hall and everyone was surprised to see Ethel deliberately sitting down next to Mildred, for it was common knowledge that the two were not on the best of terms.

'You haven't changed, I see,' remarked Ethel provokingly.

Mildred ignored this jibe and sprinkled sugar over her bowl of porridge which resembled a drought-stricken river-bed.

'Actually,' continued Ethel, 'I've got a bone to pick with you, Mildred Hubble.'

'Oh?' said Mildred. 'What?'

'It's about terrorizing my little sister,' replied Ethel.

'I don't even *know* your little sister!' exclaimed Mildred.

'Really?' said Ethel. 'Are you sure you don't remember telling a poor little girl named Sybil some stupid story about being turned into a frog?'

'Gosh, was that your sister?' asked Mildred.

'Yes, it *was*, as a matter of fact,' replied Ethel.

'I don't know why we didn't notice, Mil,' said Maud, rallying to her friend's side. 'We should have noticed that spiky nose anywhere.'

Ethel turned deep mauve with rage.

'Oh, come *on*, Ethel,' said Mildred, trying to make peace. 'It *was* only a made-up story. She *was* being a bit of a weed and in any case I went to cheer her up in the first place.'

'A fine way to cheer people up!' retorted Ethel. 'Terrifying the wits out of them. Sybil still hasn't got over the shock – and don't you go insulting my family. Sybil's delicate, not a weed.'

'*Look*, Ethel,' said Mildred firmly, 'just stop it, will you? I'm not getting into a fight over some silly little first-year whether she's your sister or not, and if you'll excuse me, this porridge is bad enough hot, but cold it's inedible and there's a long way to go till lunchtime.'

'I won't forget this,' muttered Ethel. 'No one insults *my* family and gets away with it.'

'Weed!' exclaimed Mildred, feeling suddenly reckless after all Ethel's prodding. 'All you Hallows are weeds, weeds, weeds!'

Ethel got up and flounced out of the hall, looking grim.

'You shouldn't goad her,' said Enid. 'You know what she's like.'

'I know,' said Mildred, 'but she does ask for it sometimes with all her airs and graces. "No one insults *my* family",' she mimicked in Ethel's voice. 'She's just an old windbag, she'll have forgotten by tomorrow.'

'I wouldn't be too sure about *that*,' warned Maud.

After breakfast Miss Hardbroom announced that the rest of the morning would be devoted to cat-training. All the girls were presented with black kittens in their first term at the academy and these were trained to ride on the back of their broomsticks. Mildred, however, had been given a rather dim-witted tabby because there hadn't been quite enough black ones to go round. It seemed rather typical of her luck that she had ended up with the wrong sort of cat, and she couldn't help wondering if Miss Hardbroom had made sure that the misfit kitten had been given to Mildred, rather than someone like Ethel.

'I hope you have all been practising during the holiday,' said Miss Hardbroom, as the girls all lined up with their brooms hovering next to them and the cats perched on the back – that is to say, *most* of the cats were perched on the back. Mildred's tabby was clinging desperately

to the front of her cardigan, its claws
hooked in and a wild, desperate look on
its face.

'The cat is supposed to be *on* the
broomstick, Mildred,' said Miss Hardbroom wearily.

'Yes, Miss Hardbroom,' agreed
Mildred, dragging the cat from her front
and reducing the cardigan to shreds at
the same time. The desperate creature

38

immediately spread itself flat on the back of the broom with its eyes glued shut as if awaiting execution.

'How many terms have you been training that cat, Mildred?' said Miss Hardbroom. 'Look at the other cats. None of *them* seem to be finding it so terribly difficult to just *sit* on their brooms. It is not as though they were being asked to do an aerobatic display, Mildred. Now take that cat to your room and work with it there for the rest of the morning. The creature is not fit to be seen until it is properly trained. It is a disgrace to the academy.'

'Yes, Miss Hardbroom,' said Mildred, now faced with the embarrassing task of prising the unfortunate cat from the broomstick and making her way miserably from the yard with the taunting stare of Ethel boring into her back.

Inside her room, Mildred decided to get into bed for a few minutes to warm up. It was a freezing cold day and her feet were like blocks of ice after the session in the yard. The cat, delighted that its ordeal was over, burrowed under the covers like a furry hot-water bottle, and although Mildred had only meant to sit and get warm, within a few minutes her eyelids began to droop, and before long she was fast asleep – *so* fast asleep that she did not hear the door opening very quietly.

CHAPTER FOUR

The noise of the bedroom door being slammed woke Mildred with a start. She opened her eyes and froze with horror and disbelief at the sight of a vast creature staring down at her with green eyes each as big as a lilypond.

Mildred closed her eyes again, hoping that perhaps it was only a nightmare, but when she sneaked another look, the apparition was still there, and now it began patting gently at Mildred with its gigantic paws.

Terrified, Mildred backed away and crashed into something hard, which seemed to be a huge iron railing towering above her. However, at this distance from the monster, she could see that it was none other than her own tabby cat, which for some reason had grown to the size of a mammoth.

Knowing the cat as well as she did, Mildred could see that, despite its size, it was frightened out of its wits. Her suspicions flew at once to Ethel having cast a spell on the cat to get even with Mildred for the insult to Ethel's family.

'Don't be scared, Tab,' she started to say, but much to her surprise, all that came out was a strange hoarse noise sounding rather like 'Craark!'

Panic began to grip Mildred as it slowly dawned on her that not only Tabby, but also the bedstead, all the furniture and even the bats sleeping round the picture rail were many times larger than usual. This led her to the alarming conclusion that it was not *they* who were bigger, but *she* who was smaller – and a *lot* smaller.

She peered over the edge of the bedstead and saw a cliff of bedcover stretching endlessly to the stone floor. Tabby began purring which sounded, to the miniature Mildred, like a squadron of aeroplanes taking off.

'Oh, do stop it, Tab. I can't hear myself think!' she tried to say, but once again the words seemed to stick in her throat and come out as a croak.

Mildred decided to get to the chest of drawers, on which stood a small mirror, so that she could see just how small she was. The end of the bedstead was only a few inches away from the drawers, but in her new tiny condition it appeared to be miles. However, to her great surprise, she suddenly felt the impulse to take a flying leap at the huge gap, and landed with the ease of an acrobat on top of the chest.

'How strange,' thought Mildred, 'I had no idea that I could jump like that!'

She soon discovered why, and it was

not a pleasant discovery. Looking back at her from the mirror, with eyes like saucers, was a small, olive-green frog. Mildred turned round, but there was no one behind her. She stretched out her hand and saw a green, damp limb reach out to touch the mirror-frog's webbed foot.

Mildred began to cry, and as she lifted her hand to wipe away the tears she watched with horrified fascination as the reflection did the same.

'This is no use at all,' Mildred said to herself sternly. 'Sitting here crying isn't going to change anything. I must get help.'

She jumped back onto the bed and noticed something lying on the pillow. It was a giant-sized clump of weeds, Ethel's way of telling Mildred who had cast the spell and why.

Mildred leapt to the floor and sat there for a moment, reflecting how nice it was to be able to jump such an amazing distance without getting hurt. It reminded her of the disastrous pole-vault on the school sports-day, when Enid had cast a spell on Mildred's pole to help her, but had inadvertently overdone the magic and Mildred had sailed through Miss Hardbroom's study window.

However, the ability to jump was the *only* pleasant aspect of Mildred's new condition and a sudden, hot wave of panic seized her. She felt utterly trapped in her small, cramped frog's body, her knees felt bent in the wrong place and her arms were too short, and it was quite terrifying trying to speak and only being capable of a hoarse croaking sound. There was a large gap beneath Mildred's door, and she decided to set off and find someone to help her. Watched by her baffled cat, Mildred squeezed through the

gap and hopped away down the corridor, convinced that *nothing* could be worse than just sitting helplessly in her room.

As it turned out, she would have done better to have stayed on her pillow, for there she might have been found by Maud or Enid who would possibly have put two and two together at the curious sight of a cat and frog nestling on the same bed. But outside her room, Mildred

48

was just a common frog who had strayed into the school, where it would be unlikely to occur to anyone (except the wicked person who had done the deed) that it might be a second-year witch under an enchantment.

CHAPTER FIVE

With the worst possible timing, Mildred turned the corner just as Miss Hardbroom strode through the door leading from the yard.

'Well, well,' she said, bending down and picking up the little frog, 'what have we here then?' And without further ado, she crammed Mildred into her pocket and marched off.

It was not very pleasant in the pocket. Mildred felt around in the bumping, musty darkness and discovered a whistle, a notebook with a rubber band round it, and a voluminous handkerchief.

The next thing she knew, Miss Hardbroom had pulled her out of the pocket and plonked her unceremoniously into a high-sided glass jar. Through the glass she saw that she was on a shelf in the potion laboratory and the tall figure of her formmistress was swirling out of the door.

Mildred felt absolutely dreadful. There appeared to be no way of escaping and even if she *did* escape, she had no idea what to do. She wondered if Ethel would relent and change her back, or whether she might be really wicked enough to leave her as a frog, for ever. She also wondered if Miss Hardbroom and the class would begin to wonder where she was, after a while.

They were wondering where she was

at that very moment. Miss Hardbroom had, in fact, been on her way to Mildred's room when she encountered the frog. After leaving the potion laboratory, she soon discovered that Mildred was not in her room and set off to look all over the school where, of course, she did not find the missing pupil. The class when questioned did not know where Mildred was either. It was a mystery.

'Perhaps she's run away?' suggested Enid to Maud as the girls trooped in for dinner. 'H.B. *was* cross with her about the cat.'

'I don't think so,' said Maud. 'She would have taken the cat with her if she'd done that.'

'Well, I can't think *where* she is then,' shrugged Enid.

'Nor can I,' said Maud. 'But if you ask *me*, Ethel's got something to do with it. She's got that *look* on. You know, that "*I* know something *you* don't" sort of look.'

'We'd better keep an eye on her then,' said Enid.

Meanwhile, in the potion laboratory, Mildred was desperately trying to overbalance the jar by climbing up the side and leaning on it. However, she could

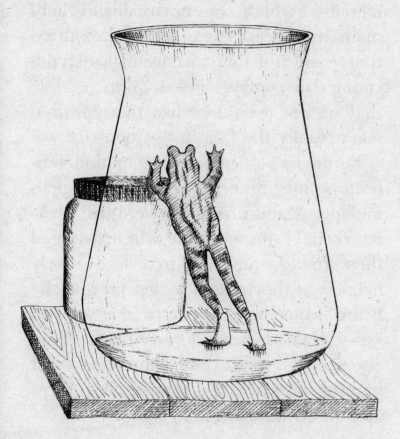

only get up a little way before she tumbled backwards, as the jar had a heavy glass base which proved impossible to overbalance. After several tries she gave up and wept a pool of panicky, frustrated tears. All she could do now was to rely on Ethel being merciful (which was not one of Ethel's main qualities). Also, Mildred realized that even if Ethel *was* feeling merciful enough to confess, it was quite possible that no one would realize that Mildred was actually the frog in the jar.

Form Two filed into the potion laboratory after dinner for an hour of spell-making. Maud and Enid were still racking their brains as to the whereabouts of their friend, and Mildred felt utterly helpless as they passed by her jar and she heard Maud say, 'Perhaps she *has* run away, Enid. I mean, I can't think where else she's gone and she knows she'll get into the most dreadful trouble if she turns up now without a good excuse.'

'I'm *here*!' Mildred tried to shriek, but it only came out as a frenzied croaking.

'That is the noisiest frog I've ever had in this laboratory,' snapped Miss Hard-broom with a piercing glance at the jar. Mildred lapsed into silence and fixed her eyes on Maud in the hope that she might be able to send some sort of message through the air – like a radio wave – to her friend. It almost succeeded.

'Enid,' said Maud, as they sorted through the ingredients for an invisibility potion, 'I'm sure that frog's staring at me. It hasn't taken its eyes off our table for the last ten minutes.'

'Don't be silly,' said Enid, 'frogs don't stare at people.'

'Well, that one does,' said Maud. 'Look!'

Enid looked. The little frog was definitely gazing hard in Maud's direction, and when it saw Enid turn to look, it began jumping up and down and croaking like a mad thing.

'Maud,' said Miss Hardbroom, 'would you please remove that frog from the jar and put it into the box in the cupboard? We do not wish to listen to *that* noise all afternoon.'

'CRAARK!' pleaded Mildred. 'CRAARK! CRAAARK! CRAA-AARK!' Maud approached the shelf cautiously, reached into the jar, and took Mildred out.

Mildred gave one last, long look into Maud's eyes, but she could see that there was no hope of Maud recognizing a half-mad frog as her best friend. There was nothing for it but to flee.

Mildred leapt into the air as high as her new, powerful legs would take her, and landed with a soft 'splat' on Maud and Enid's bench.

'Don't just *stand* there, girls!' bellowed Miss Hardbroom. 'Catch the creature!'

The entire class took off in pursuit of the frog as it sprang nimbly from bench to bench. Hands clutched and faces loomed, and suddenly Mildred remembered that the class would be making an invisibility potion. (Miss Hardbroom had told them to revise for it after breakfast.) Mildred dived for Ethel's bench, knowing that Ethel would have made the best potion of all, and there it was, dark green and bubbling in the cauldron, with a half-full test-tube conveniently spilling a puddle of the liquid onto the bench. Mildred's frog-tongue shot out and lapped as much as it could.

'Oh, Miss Hardbroom!' she heard Ethel cry. 'The frog's disappeared!'

Mildred heaved a sigh of relief and leapt onto the floor where she huddled in perfect silence under the bookcase near the door.

'How very strange,' mused Miss Hard-broom, 'not only the noisiest, but also the most knowledgeable frog I have ever been privileged to meet.'

'I'm sure it was trying to tell me something,' whispered Maud to Enid. 'Perhaps it knows something about Mildred?'

'What could a *frog* know?' asked Enid.

Maud shrugged her shoulders. '*I* don't know,' she replied, 'but it was no ordinary frog. I can tell you *that* for certain.'

CHAPTER SIX

owering beneath the book-case, Mildred dared not move in case she had begun to be visible again. (When you have taken an invisibility potion, you reappear very gradually, head first, followed by the rest of the body.)

In fact, being invisible is a very odd sensation indeed. Imagine holding out your leg and feeling it with your invisible hand while being unable actually to see it. For this reason, walking becomes rather a difficult experience as you can feel your feet moving along but cannot see where they are going. This means that you often find yourself moving in the opposite direction to the one intended which, of course, is extremely annoying.

Mildred held out her arm to see if it had begun to reappear but it hadn't. Her patience paid off at last when she heard Miss Hardbroom tell the girls to pack up their books, and after much clattering and bustling, the door closed and the laboratory fell silent.

Mildred hopped out and looked around. As usual, there was a gap of several inches under the door. In fact, it seemed to be a school speciality that none of the doors fitted properly and the windows (most of which were slit windows) had no glass in them at all. The whole school seemed to have been designed with the sole purpose of freezing all the pupils to death.

Mildred squeezed through the gap and set off as fast as possible along the corridor and down the spiral staircase to the yard. From there she hopped to the pond at the back of the school, for she felt sure that she could hide safely there in the weeds and rushes while she tried to find some solution to her appalling problem.

Sitting on a stone in the middle of the water was the large frog that Mildred had often seen, and which had been the inspiration for the tale which had scared Ethel's sister.

'Craark!' it said, and to Mildred's delight, she found that she could understand what the creature meant. It said, 'What on earth's the matter with you? Where's the rest of your body?'

Mildred realized that her head had reappeared, which must have looked rather alarming, bobbing about all over the place with no body attached.

'Don't be afraid,' said Mildred. 'I've taken an invisibility potion and I'm just coming back into view. You'll be able to see all of me in a moment.'

'Where did you get the potion from?' asked the frog, slipping silently from the stone and swimming across to Mildred's head.

'Oh dear,' said Mildred, 'it's a long story. I'm not really a frog at all. I'm a second-year witch at the school, and this beastly girl called Ethel Hallow has changed me into a frog and I was –'

'Good gracious me!' exclaimed the frog. 'This is quite amazing! *I'm* not a frog either. I'm a magician. What a wonderful coincidence. I've been here for years and this is the first conversation I've had with a human for simply ages. How extraordinary! Well, well, well, I can scarcely believe it. Allow me to offer you a nice fly from my store.'

'A *fly*?' repeated Mildred.

'Oh dear,' said the frog-magician. 'Of course, you've only been a frog for a while. A *fly*, my dear, you know, bzzzzzz. They really are quite delicious once you get used to the idea. I nearly starved at first because I couldn't bear the idea of eating – well – insects and the like, but it's amazing what you can get used to.'

Mildred grimaced. 'I'm hoping to be changed back before I get used to it,' she said (with considerable spirit, bearing in mind how hopeless she felt). 'Tell me how you got here in the first place.'

'Well, my dear,' said the frog-magician, settling fatly onto a stone. 'It was so long ago that I've almost forgotten. Let me see . . . Yes, well in those days, of course, the castle was not a school. It was used for meetings and conferences of magicians. We used to have a lovely "do" in the summer. Like a holiday camp it was, endless teas and lectures and displays of magic all afternoon. Anyway, to cut a long story short, I had an argument – rather like *you* did, by the sound of it – with a fellow magician and this was the result. Before I could persuade him to change his mind, the summer was over, everyone went home and I was left behind. I've been here ever since. I must admit I get very glum sometimes.' He breathed a huge sigh and gazed into the dark water.

'Why don't you come with *me*?' said Mildred brightly. 'I'm going to find my friend Maud, after dark. I know I can make her understand, and then she'll be able to help me. She'll help you, too.'

A large tear splashed from the frog-magician's eye. 'It's no use,' he croaked sadly. 'It's got to be a magician who takes off the spell. There aren't any in the school, are there?'

'No, there aren't,' said Mildred thoughtfully. 'All right then, I'll go to find Maud by myself, but I'll come back for you as soon as I'm changed back and I'll get you to a magician somehow. I won't forget.'

'You're very kind, my dear – What is your name?' said the frog-magician.

'Mildred Hubble,' replied Mildred. 'What's yours?'

'Algernon er – something-or-other Webb. Isn't that awful?' said the frog-magician. 'Do you know I can't re-member the first bit, I've been here so long. What was it now? Bowen-Webb? Stone-Webb? Or was it Webbley-Stone? I'm sorry, child, I've completely forgot-ten. Oh dear, it was all so very long ago. I must say, sometimes I'd give *anything* to have a proper old-fashioned tea again, one gets so fed-up with flies and water-boatmen. Every now and then I can see it all so clearly: a nice log fire and a little round table with a tablecloth, and hot toast with great slabs of butter, and crumpets with honey all oozing out of the little holes, and a china cup with steaming tea –'

The memory was too much for him and he erupted into loud, desperate sobs, a pitiful sound to hear.

Mildred hopped next to him and patted him with a half-visible arm. 'Don't

cry, Mr Algernon, sir,' she said comfortingly. 'You *shall* have crumpets for tea again, don't you worry. It'll be all right, I promise it will.'

CHAPTER SEVEN

Night had fallen and the pupils of the academy were all in bed. That is to say *most* of the pupils were in bed. Enid had sneaked into Maud's room for a quick conference about Mildred. It was bitterly cold in the cell-like bedroom and the two girls were huddled on the bed, wrapped in blankets, with cats draped over their feet to keep out the cold. (Maud was taking care of Mildred's tabby.)

'Well, I give up,' said Enid. 'If she *has* run away, she's left every single piece of clothing behind – even her cardigan, so she must be frozen solid by now.'

'She *hasn't* run away,' said Maud. '*She* wouldn't have gone just because H.B. told her off. Anyway, she's not likely to have

run away without old Tabby here, especially as that was *why* H.B. was cross in the first place. It just doesn't make sense. No, *I'm* quite sure that Ethel knows something about it. Don't you remember what she said to Mildred? "No one insults *my* family and gets away with it." Well *I* think she's done something really awful to Mildred.'

'Like what?' asked Enid.

Just at that moment, the cats all leapt to their feet with their fur on end and looked in the direction of the door. The girls exchanged nervous glances, thinking that it must be Miss Hardbroom come to reprimand them for being out of bed. Maud crept to the door and opened it very slowly.

Outside in the shadowy corridor was the little frog which had escaped from the potion laboratory. Maud and Enid could tell it was the same one because its feet had not yet reappeared.

Mildred hopped inside and was picked up by Maud, who took her over to Enid.

Tabby immediately began nuzzling up against the frog in a very friendly way, unlike the other two cats who kept in the background, backs arched and humming frantically.

'How strange, Enid!' said Maud. 'Look

at Tabby. It seems as if they've met before.'

The two witches suddenly looked at each other in horror.

'Oh *no!*' they exclaimed at the same time.

'It can't be!' gasped Maud. 'Or can it?'

'I think it might be,' replied Enid grimly. She took the frog from Maud and held it up near her face.

'Are you –' she began, but before she could finish, the little frog was leaping up and down, nodding its head and croaking so loudly that the girls were afraid someone would hear.

'Sssh!' whispered Enid. 'Calm down, for goodness' sake. Now then, are you our very good friend, Mildred Hubble?'

There was no doubt about it, from the nodding and mad capering, that here was the answer to Mildred's sudden disappearance.

'Did Ethel do it?' asked Maud.

More nodding and croaking was the answer.

'*Right*!' said Maud. 'Come on, Enid.'

Ethel was not asleep, either. She was sitting up in bed learning the chant which was to be tested the next day. She nearly leapt through the ceiling when the door opened and Maud and Enid marched menacingly into the room.

'Recognize this?' asked Maud, holding out the frog. 'Remind you of anyone, does it?'

Ethel turned as white as a sheet. 'I – I don't know *what* you're talking about,' she said.

'All right,' said Maud, 'then we're off to Miss Hardbroom. Come on, Enid. Sorry to have bothered you, Ethel.'

'No!' cried Ethel. 'It's *Mildred*, isn't it? Oh, thank goodness you found her. I didn't *mean* her to run off and get lost. I just wanted to give her a fright, that's all.

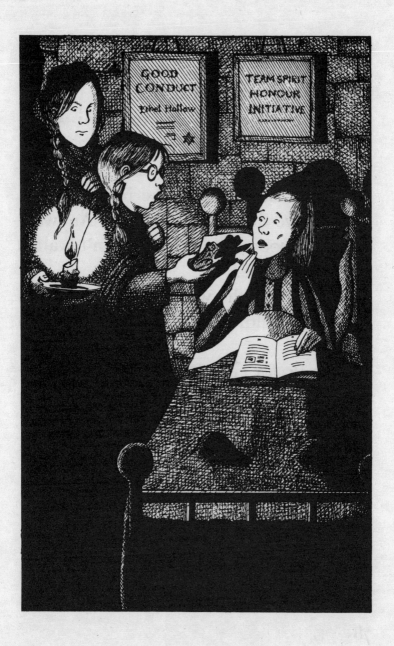

Come here and let me take off the spell.'

'Hold on a moment,' said Enid, 'I think we'd *better* get Miss Hardbroom. I mean, how are we going to explain where Mildred's been?'

'Let's tell her in the morning,' wheedled Ethel. 'She'll be in a dreadful mood if we disturb her tonight. Anyway, I'm sure poor Mildred here can't wait a moment longer.'

Ethel spoke the words of the spell, and at once Mildred was standing before them.

'Thanks for nothing, Ethel Hallow,' she said, rubbing her arms and legs. 'Gosh, it feels really odd to be this big again. Oh, Maud, it was so awful in the potion lab, I really thought I'd had it.'

The door opened like a thunderclap, and there stood Miss Hardbroom.

'Having a little party are we, girls?' she inquired drily. 'Ah, Mildred, I see you've decided to rejoin us at last. We hope you have had a pleasant time wherever you have been. Would it be too much, perhaps, to inquire exactly where you *have* been. Hmm?'

The three friends looked desperately at Ethel who stepped forward with a smirk flickering at the corners of her mouth.

'I caught Mildred creeping down the corridor with Maud and Enid here,' she said innocently. 'So I invited them into my room and I was just coming to fetch you, Miss Hardbroom.'

'*Ethel*!' exclaimed Maud, Enid and Mildred together.

'That's not *true*, Miss Hardbroom,' squeaked Mildred indignantly. 'Ethel turned me into a frog and that's where I've been for the last day, and it was *her* fault. She's only just changed me back.'

'I did *not*,' lied Ethel, sounding convincingly angry. 'I wouldn't *do* such a thing – unlike some people around here,' she added under her breath, referring to the time when Mildred had accidently changed Ethel into a pig during their first term at the school.

'Mildred,' said Miss Hardbroom, 'you will write out five hundred times, in perfect handwriting, "I must learn to curb my imagination and to – " good gracious, girl! What on earth has happened to your feet?'

They all looked and saw that Mildred's feet, still recovering from the invisibility potion, had not yet reappeared, even

though she had changed back to her usual self.

'That *proves* it!' exclaimed Mildred joyfully. 'Miss Hardbroom, *I* was the frog in the potion laboratory, the one you found in the corridor, and the potion I took is only just wearing off, that's why I haven't any feet at the moment. Oh yes! And to prove it even more, I can tell you that you have a handkerchief, a whistle and a notebook with a rubber band round it in your pocket!'

Miss Hardbroom turned to Ethel.

'*Well*?' she asked, in tones so terrifying that all four of her pupils shrank back against the wall.

'I – I, well – I – she *had* insulted my f-family, Miss Hardb-broom,' said Ethel feebly. 'And I really didn't mean her to run off like that. I only meant to give her a scare. I didn't mean . . .' She trailed into silence.

'Ethel, Mildred,' said Miss Hard-broom, 'you will both come to my room first thing in the morning before break-fast. Now get along to bed at once, all of you.'

Their form-mistress ushered the three friends to their separate rooms. Mildred's room was the last of all.

'Let us hope that your feet are in the correct place by the morning, Mildred,' said Miss Hardbroom frostily, as Mildred hastened inside and closed the door.

CHAPTER EIGHT

Shortly after the rising bell had been rung, Ethel and Mildred were waiting anxiously outside Miss Hardbroom's door. It was the first time that Ethel had been summoned to her formmistress for any reason other than praise.

'It's *your* fault, Mildred Hubble,' she muttered, as they paced up and down the corridor. 'If you hadn't told that stupid story to Sybil and upset her, I wouldn't have done it to you. Anyway, I really *was* going to take the spell off straight away, but of course *you* have to go hopping off and get caught and land us in this mess.'

'*You've* got a nerve, Ethel Hallow!' said Mildred. 'You just can't ever admit you might be wrong, can you? It wasn't exactly *fun* being pursued round the potion lab and shoved into jars. It wouldn't occur to you that –'

The door opened and Miss Hardbroom beckoned them inside.

'Sit,' she barked, indicating two chairs opposite her desk. They all sat down.

'It *wasn't* my fault, Miss Hardbroom!' Ethel blurted out. 'Mildred Hubble told my little sister this story about first-years being changed into frogs by the teachers. She even told Sybil that the frog in the school *pond* was enchanted, and poor Sybil was in such a state that I thought someone ought to teach Mildred a lesson.'

'It wasn't exactly like that, Miss Hardbroom,' said Mildred. 'I'd gone up to Ethel's sister to cheer her up because she was looking so miserable. I didn't know –'

'I have heard quite enough excuses,' interrupted Miss Hardbroom, 'and I do not wish to hear any more. Frankly, I am not in the least bit interested in whose fault the incident was.

'The reason I have called you both here is to remind you that you are now second-year witches, and I do not expect this ridiculous feud between you two girls to continue. Do you understand?'

'Yes, Miss Hardbroom,' replied Ethel and Mildred meekly.

'Ethel,' continued Miss Hardbroom, 'just because you happen to be an excel-

lent scholar and one of the most helpful
members of my class, I do not expect you
to lie your way out of a situation when it
has become awkward. Do you understand
this?'

'Yes, Miss Hardbroom,' said Ethel.

'Neither,' said Miss Hardbroom, 'do I
expect you to contravene the Witches'
Code, rule number seven, paragraph two,
by changing your fellows into any sort of
animal for what*ever* reason. Do you
understand *that*?'

88

'Yes, Miss Hardbroom,' said Ethel.

'Good,' said Miss Hardbroom, 'then you will understand why I am giving you one hundred lines which will say "I must tell the truth at all times."'

She turned her attention to Mildred. 'Mildred, I would ask you to refrain from tormenting the first-years with untrue horror stories about the academy, and to make some attempt to *think* – if that is possible – before you embark upon any more madcap escapades.'

'Yes, Miss Hardbroom,' replied Mildred. 'Oh, and Miss Hardbroom, I've just remembered, there *is* a frog in the pond and it really *is* someone under enchantment. I *know* it sounds like another made-up story –'

'Mildred Hubble,' said Miss Hard-broom wearily, 'what have I just said to you? No, don't attempt to answer. I expect you've completely forgotten already, haven't you? Sometimes I feel that any attempt to communicate with you is an utter waste of time.

'Now I have said all that I wish to say to you girls except, Mildred, that you will write one hundred lines which will say, "I must try very hard not to be quite so silly." Now hurry along to breakfast, girls. That will be all.'

Mildred was now faced with the impossible task of convincing someone that there was an elderly magician in the pond. She tried to tell Maud and Enid, but they had had enough of frog stories, particularly as Mildred had actually admitted to them, at the time, that the story she had told Sybil was not true.

It seemed quite hopeless. The only way of getting to a magician was at the celebrations on Hallowe'en night, but after the broomstick display, which Mildred had ruined the year before, she felt very worried about creating any more havoc in that direction.

Mildred spent a lot of time by the pond telling the frog-magician that she hadn't forgotten him and that she would get him out if it was the last thing she did. He always kept a distance from her, but she felt sure he knew who she was. Looking at his froggy face, half-submerged in the murky water, it was hard to believe that he really was anything more than an ordinary frog, and Mildred could see why no one had recognized her when she was in the same plight.

CHAPTER NINE

A week before the Hallowe'en celebration, Miss Hardbroom entered the classroom, looking grim.

'Sit, girls,' she said, looking round severely at the rows of pupils. 'I have here a letter from the chief magician, Mr Hellibore, who presides over the Hallowe'en festivities each year. In this letter he specifically requests that the girls respons- ible for the utter fiasco, which *should* have been our broomstick display last year, are to be kept away from this year's display so that he can relax and enjoy the events taking place. Those two girls were Ethel Hallow and Mildred Hubble. It is true that the incident was not actually Mildred's fault, for once, because Ethel *had* cast a spell on the broomstick which Mildred was using, but in view of our little *chat* this morning, girls –' here she darted a glance at Ethel and Mildred who wriggled uncomfortably in their seats – 'I feel this is a most fitting punishment for both of you. As you retire to your beds at dusk on the eve of Hallowe'en, perhaps you might ponder upon the exciting evening you *could* have been enjoying and resolve to end this ridiculous feud at last.'

Mildred was very upset at her exclusion from Hallowe'en for several reasons. One was the awful unfairness of it all, as it really hadn't been her fault that Ethel had cast a bad spell on the broomstick she had lent to Mildred, thus ruining the display. Also it would be very hard to stay in bed and miss the evening's fun. But, worst of all, she would not be able to take her unfortunate friend to be changed back to his normal self, and this was the only night of the whole year when she would be in the presence of a magician.

There was only one thing to do. She would have to persuade someone to change places with her, and if that didn't work she would have to kidnap someone and *force* them to swap places. Even the thought of this plan seemed dreadful to Mildred, who could see how such a course of action was fraught with danger, but there really was no alternative if she was to help the frog-magician.

Maud and Enid were the obvious people to ask but they flatly refused.

'You must be barmy, Mildred,' exclaimed Maud. 'H.B. would *slaughter* us if we got caught. Anyway what's it *for*? I mean if *I* was you I'd just put up with it and stay in bed. Enid and I will describe it all when we come back.'

'Look, Maud,' pleaded Mildred, 'I *know* it's hard for you to believe me, but that frog in the pond really *is* a magician and he can only be changed back by another magician. If you don't want to change places with me, then couldn't you take him yourself and ask the chief magician for help? *Please*.'

'No fear!' said Maud and Enid together.

'Honestly, Mil,' said Enid gently, 'I know it must have been awful when you were turned into a frog, what with the narrow squeak in the potion lab and everything, but don't you think perhaps you're getting a little *obsessed* with frogs and ponds? Maud and I have seen you down there chatting away to the empty water. Perhaps a nice evening in bed might be good for you, after all.'

Mildred stomped away feeling desperate. If Maud and Enid thought she was mad and wouldn't help her, then no one would and the only course of action was to go ahead with the kidnapping plan. Mildred quailed at the prospect.

The morning of the celebrations dawned and the whole day was given over to ironing best robes, practising on broomsticks and chanting. Mildred and Ethel sat miserably at their desks, feeling very left out of all the bustle.

As the afternoon drew to a close, Mildred crept downstairs and out into the darkening yard. She hurried to the pond and peered among the reeds to see if her friend was visible.

'Mr Algernon, sir,' she whispered, 'come out, Mr Algernon. I've got something to tell you, sir.'

For a moment the water lay dark and still, then a ripple touched the surface and two green eyes appeared like periscopes.

'Oh, Mr Algernon!' exclaimed Mildred with relief, and before he had time to hide away under a stone, as he usually did, she shot a hand into the water and scooped him up. He did not want to be

caught at all, and although Mildred told
him where they were going and tried to
soothe him, he struggled madly and
looked at her with great suspicion.
Mildred slid him carefully into her
pocket and raced up the stairs to her
room, where she transferred him to a
small box with holes in the lid which she
had prepared specially for the journey.

'You'll be all right there for a while,'
she told him, tying on the lid with a piece
of string. 'You mustn't worry. It'll be all
right I promise.'

The next step was to find and kidnap a suitable victim. Of course, the easiest thing to do would have been to change someone into a frog or snail or some other small creature which could easily be kept hidden in a box until she returned. But, to be honest, Mildred felt that there had been quite enough animal enchantments in the school to last a lifetime, and it seemed a less desperate measure to do a nice, straightforward kidnap where at least you could see exactly what was happening.

As she came out of her room, Mildred saw a third-year witch named Griselda Blackwood approaching down the corridor, carrying her cat.

'Excuse me!' gasped Mildred. 'Er – I was wondering if you could just come and help me for a moment?'

'Whatever for?' asked Griselda. 'What's the matter, Mildred? You look quite pale.'

'There's something horrible under my bed!' exclaimed Mildred. 'Could you come and help me get it out?'

'Something horrible?' repeated Griselda, drawing back in alarm. 'Why, what do you mean *something horrible*? You can't really expect me to go fishing about underneath your bed if I don't even know what I might find under it, now can you?'

'It's a er – beetle!' replied Mildred triumphantly. 'I've got this *thing* about beetles. A horrid brown one with pincers ran up my pyjama leg once and I've never got over it. Please help me, Griselda. I won't get a wink of sleep otherwise.'

'A beetle!' laughed Griselda. 'Is that all? I thought it must be a tarantula at least with all the fuss you're making. Come on, then.'

While Griselda was half under the bed, feeling about, Mildred very stealthily tied her bootlaces together.

'I can't seem to find anything,' said Griselda, shuffling out and sitting back on her heels.

As quick as a flash, Mildred pulled out a lasso of rope which she had hidden in a drawer and slipped it over the astonished girl's head and shoulders, yanking it tightly enough to bind her arms to her sides. Before the poor victim had a chance to scream, Mildred had tied a gag around her mouth. As a last resort, Griselda tried to run for it, but of course her bootlaces were tied together so she fell flat on her back.

'I'm really ever so sorry to do this to you,' apologized Mildred humbly, as she tied Griselda's ankles together with her sash. 'It's really in a very good cause and I'll explain everything to you later when I get back. I'm so sorry, I really am. I don't usually go around doing this sort of thing. I hope you don't mind *too* dreadfully.'

Griselda stared up at Mildred from the floor with horror.

'Mmmmmmmm!' she raged through the gag. 'Mm-mmm, mmmm-mm, mm, mm, mm, mm, mmmm!'

Mildred pulled some bedclothes from her bed and covered Griselda tenderly.

'There really isn't any point in shouting,' said Mildred, putting a pillow underneath the victim's head. 'No one can hear you. They're all getting ready in the playground. I'll borrow your cat if you don't mind. Mine's awful on a broom and anyway it's too easy to recognize.'

Mildred changed from her ordinary school uniform to the best robes which the girls always wore for special occasions. She unplaited her hair and shook it out loose. (The whole school, including the teachers, always wore their hair loose when they dressed in their best robes.) She put on her cape and turned up the collar and pulled her hat low over her eyes.

There was a soft 'meeow' from the top of the wardrobe, and Mildred saw her little tabby cat watching reproachfully as she prepared to go without it.

'Oh, Tabby,' said Mildred, reaching up and tickling its chin, 'I can't take you or the whole school will recognize us.'

She picked up the box with the frog-magician in it and wedged it into her cape pocket. Then she slung Griselda's cat around her shoulders and took her broomstick from its place against the wall.

'Good-bye, Griselda,' said Mildred, slinking out of the room feeling like a criminal. 'I won't be long and then I'll explain everything and you won't be cross any more.'

CHAPTER TEN

ut of the window, as she hastened down the spiral staircase, Mildred saw the fires which were being lit in the ruins of the old castle where the celebrations were always held. Her heart pounded as she joined the throng of girls in the gloomy yard, all looking most dramatic with their hair loose and their long black robes and witches' hats.

'Thank goodness, it's almost dark,' thought Mildred, tagging on to the end of Form Three as their form-mistress counted them all.

'Is everyone accounted for?' asked Miss Cackle.

All the form-mistresses answered 'yes' in turn, and the pupils began their flight to the castle.

The school receded into the distance as the pupils skimmed above the treetops, and Mildred was grateful that no talking was allowed in flight, so nobody could ask her any awkward questions. The borrowed cat was a wonderful balancer, and Mildred felt rather disloyal as she found herself thinking how nice it would be to have a well-behaved sleek black cat which she could feel proud of.

Back at the academy, Ethel sat fuming in bed and watched from her window as the pupils rose like a flock of bats into the twilight and sailed away without her. She

picked up her candle and decided to go along to Mildred's room and have a grumble at her.

Outside Mildred's room, Ethel pressed her ear against the door and was surprised to hear a strange noise from within.

'Mildred?' called Ethel, knocking softly. The noise grew louder.

'Mmmmmm! Mmmm, mm, mmm!'

Ethel opened the door and held up her

candle to reveal the awful sight of Mildred's victim trussed up on the floor.

'What on earth has happened to you?' gasped Ethel, untying the gag and pulling at the knots in the sash and rope.

'It's that Mildred Hubble!' said Griselda, who was almost in tears. 'She must have gone berserk. She got me in here under false pretences, tied me up, stole my cat and went to the display in my place. Honestly, Ethel, she sounded really mad, wittering on about beetles up her pyjama leg and suchlike. Whatever shall we do?'

'Go after her, of course!' answered Ethel, delighted at the thought of the praise they would get when they revealed Mildred's wicked behaviour.

'Come on, Griselda, I'll change into my outdoor clothes and meet you in the yard with my broom in five minutes. We'll have to hurry. Goodness knows what that girl is planning!'

'All right,' agreed Griselda. 'I'll run and fetch my broom.'

Meanwhile, the academy was alighting on the castle hillside and being welcomed by the chief magician and all the other witches and magicians. The chief magi-

cian, Mr Hellibore, looked most imposing in his purple robe embroidered with moons and stars and a tall, pointed hat. Mildred would have been absolutely thrilled by it all if she had not been so terrified of the task ahead of her.

There was a long delay between the pupils' arrival and the commencement of the displays and chanting, during which Miss Cackle and the teachers greeted friends and acquaintances, and the girls all stood to attention, being neat and well-behaved and a credit to the school.

Suddenly there was a commotion in the sky and everyone looked up to see Ethel and Griselda swooping down on their brooms, waving and shouting.

'Mildred Hubble's down there!' shrieked Ethel.

'She kidnapped me!' yelled Griselda. 'And she tied me up, so she could come in my place!'

'That's enough now, girls, thank you,' ordered Miss Cackle, who was not at all pleased at such unseemly shrieking from her girls.

Miss Hardbroom strode across to the rows of pupils and Mildred pulled her hat even lower over her face. From under the brim she could see the chief magician nearby, looking rather puzzled at all the shouting.

'If you *are* here, Mildred,' said Miss Hardbroom, 'I would advise you to step forward at *once* and explain yourself.'

The pupils all began looking round at each other and Mildred knew there was little time before someone recognized her. There was no alternative but to make a dash to the magician before anyone could catch her. Summoning every scrap of courage, Mildred suddenly barged through the rows of pupils and threw herself in front of Mr Hellibore.

'Please forgive me, Your Honour,' she said, thrusting the box containing her friend into his hands. 'I know you didn't want me to come here tonight, but there is an enchanted magician in that box and I promised him that I would get him to

you so that you could change him back. I'm so sorry to cause such a lot of trouble but I didn't know what else to do.'

'What on earth is all this nonsense about?' asked the chief magician sternly. 'And are my eyes deceiving me or are you not the girl who *ruined* the broomstick display last year? If so –'

'We do apologize most humbly, Your Honour,' grovelled Miss Hardbroom, seizing Mildred's arm in a vice-like grip. 'The girl seems to have taken leave of her senses –'

'I *haven't*, Miss Hardbroom!' interrupted Mildred. '*Please*, Your Honour, Mr Hellibore, sir, it really *is* a magician. His name is Algernon Webb-something, Stonely-Webb, oh *something* like that, only he couldn't quite remember. He's been a frog for simply ages.'

'Good gracious me!' exclaimed Mr Hellibore. 'Do you know, Miss Hardbroom, it might just be Algernon Rowan-

Webb. He was my room-mate in the days when your school was used as a sort of summer camp for magicians and he actually *did* disappear one day and we all thought he must have gone home. But it was *decades* ago – why the poor chap! If you'll excuse me, Miss Hardbroom.'

Mildred kept her eyes firmly closed as the chief magician opened the box and intoned the release spell. Suddenly there was a gasp from the crowd. Mildred opened her eyes and breathed a huge sigh of relief.

Standing in front of them was an extremely old man with a beard that trailed on the ground and long flowing white hair. He was very bent over and was rubbing his eyes as if he couldn't quite believe it.

'*Algy*, old chap!' exclaimed the chief magician with joy. 'It's *Egbert*, your old friend, don't you remember?'

'Egbert!' replied Algernon. 'Yes, of

course I remember, though you were a lot younger in those days. Excuse me a moment, I shall have to sit down. It's all a bit much for me after all these years as a frog. My legs and arms feel awfully cramped. Egbert Hellibore! Well, well, what a piece of luck.'

'The luck came from your little friend here,' said Mr Hellibore, placing a hand on Mildred's shoulder. 'This child braved all our displeasure to bring you here.'

Mildred felt very shy as the vast crowd fell silent and every pair of eyes swivelled in her direction.

'Do you remember me, Mr Rowan-Webb, sir?' asked Mildred. 'We were frogs together.'

'*Remember* you?' repeated Algernon. 'My dear Mildred, how could I ever forget you. No one ever had a truer friend. Without your help I would have been a frog for ever. And please call me Algernon.'

'Well, Miss Hardbroom,' said Mr Hellibore, 'we can hardly send the girl back to school again after this act of heroism, now can we?'

Miss Hardbroom ground her teeth and managed a horribly false smile. 'Whatever you wish, Your Honour,' she replied.

'Is there anything you would like as a reward, my child?' asked Mr Hellibore, smiling kindly down at Mildred.

Mildred thought for a moment. 'Oh yes, sir!' she replied. 'There *is* one thing.'

She stepped forward on tiptoe and whispered in his ear.

'Is that *all*?' said Mr Hellibore with a laugh. He leaned across and quietly told the ancient magician what Mildred had asked for. Algernon smiled dreamily. 'What a wonderful memory you have, my dear,' he said. 'Yes, that would be very nice, very nice indeed.'

The crowd watched in fascinated

silence as Mr Hellibore snapped his fingers and a small table appeared in his hand set with a white table-cloth, tea for three, and a huge plate of toast, crumpets and butter. Algernon peered at the table, then snapped *his* fingers and a pot of honey appeared. 'Mustn't forget *that*,' he commented as he set it on the table and, with a glow of pride, Mildred walked away arm-in-arm with the two most important people at the celebrations, to have a proper old-fashioned tea by the nearest bonfire.